A Little Princess Story

I Want to Win!

Tony Ross

Andersen Press

The Little Princess liked to win.

At the castle sports day, she entered the running race.

But after just a few metres she was out of puff.

"Stop!" she commanded the other runners.

"The race must be run in the opposite direction!"

Then she turned round and sprinted back to the start line.
"I've won!" she cried.

"I want to win!" she said when she played games at home,
and since everyone lost on purpose, she usually did.

But at school it was different.
There were cups there for everything . . .

. . . and the Little Princess wanted to win them all!

She tried her HARDEST at numbers,

but her cousin won the Numbers Cup.

She tried her HARDEST at painting,

but Polly won the Painting Cup.

She tried her HARDEST at writing her poem,

but Poppy won the Poem Cup.

She tried her HARDEST at science,

but Darren won the Science Cup.

"It's not fair!" sobbed the Little Princess. "I've tried my very hardest, but I haven't won anything!"

When all the big cups had been taken from the shelf . . .

. . . there was just one little one left that nobody had noticed.

But it turned out to be the best cup of all, because it was for . . .

. . . TRYING THE HARDEST, and because she *had* tried so hard, the Little Princess won it fair and square!